HELLO, I'M THEA!

I'm *Geronimo Stilton*'s sister. As I'm sure you know from my brother's bestselling novels, I'm a special correspondent for *The Rodent's Gazette*, Mouse Island's most famous newspaper. Unlike my 'fraidy mouse brother, I absolutely adore traveling, having adventures, and meeting rodents from all around the world!

The adventure I want to tell you about begins at Mouseford Academy, the school I went to when I was a young mouseling. I had such a great experience there as a student that I came back to teach a journalism class.

When I returned as a grown mouse, I met five really special students: Colette, Nicky, Pamela, Paulina, and Violet. You could hardly imagine five more different mouselings, but they became great friends right away. And they liked me so much that they decided to name their group after me: the Thea Sisters! I was so touched by that, I decided to write about their adventures. So turn the page to read a fabumouse adventure about the

THEA SISTERS!

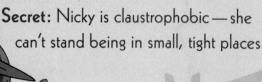

Name: Nicky

Nickname: Nic

Home: Australia

Secret ambition: Wants to be an ecologist.

Loves: Open spaces and nature.

Strengths: She is always in a good mood, as long as she's outdoors!

Weaknesses: She can't sit still!

Secret: Nicky is claustrophobic—she can't stand being in small, tight places.

Nicky

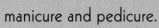
COLETTE

Name: Colette

Nickname: It's Colette, please. (She can't stand nicknames.)

Home: France

Secret ambition: Colette is very particular about her appearance. She wants to be a fashion writer.

Loves: The color pink.

Strengths: She's energetic and full of great ideas.

Weaknesses: She's always late!

Secret: To relax, there's nothing Colette likes more than a manicure and pedicure.

Colette

Name: Violet
Nickname: Vi
Home: China
Secret ambition: Wants to become a great violinist.
Loves: Books! She is a real intellectual, just like my brother, Geronimo.
Strengths: She's detail-oriented and always open to new things.
Weaknesses: She is a bit sensitive and can't stand being teased. And if she doesn't get enough sleep, she can be a real grouch!
Secret: She likes to unwind by listening to classical music and drinking green tea.

Violet

Name: Paulina
Nickname: Polly
Home: Peru
Secret ambition: Wants to be a scientist.
Loves: Traveling and meeting people from all over the world. She is also very close to her sister, Maria.
Strengths: Loves helping other rodents.
Weaknesses: She's shy and can be a bit clumsy.
Secret: She is a computer genius!

PAULINA

PAULINA

Name: Pamela
Nickname: Pam
Home: Tanzania

PAMELA

Secret ambition: Wants to become a sports journalist or a car mechanic.
Loves: Pizza, pizza, and more pizza! She'd eat pizza for breakfast if she could.
Strengths: She is a peacemaker. She can't stand arguments.
Weaknesses: She is very impulsive.
Secret: Give her a screwdriver and any mechanical problem will be solved!

Pamela

Geronimo Stilton

Thea Stilton
AND THE GREAT TULIP HEIST

Scholastic Inc.

No part of this publication may be reproduced, stored in a retrieval system, or transmitted in any form or by any means, electronic, mechanical, photocopying, recording, or otherwise without written permission from the copyright holder. For information regarding permission, please contact: Atlantyca S.p.A., Via Leopardi 8, 20123 Milan, Italy; e-mail foreignrights@atlantyca.it, www.atlantyca.com.

ISBN 978-0-545-55628-6

Copyright © 2013 by Edizioni Piemme S.p.A., Corso Como 15, 20154 Milan, Italy.

International Rights © Atlantyca S.p.A.

English translation © 2014 by Atlantyca S.p.A.

GERONIMO STILTON and THEA STILTON names, characters, and related indicia are copyright, trademark, and exclusive license of Atlantyca S.p.A. All rights reserved. The moral right of the author has been asserted.

Based on an original idea by Elisabetta Dami.

www.geronimostilton.com

Published by Scholastic Inc., 557 Broadway, New York, NY 10012. SCHOLASTIC and associated logos are trademarks and/or registered trademarks of Scholastic Inc.

Stilton is the name of a famous English cheese. It is a registered trademark of the Stilton Cheese Makers' Association. For more information, go to www.stiltoncheese.com.

Text by Thea Stilton
Original title *Sulle tracce del tulipano nero*
Cover by Giuseppe Facciotto (drawings) and Flavio Ferron (color)
Illustrations by Barbara Pellizzari (drawings) and
Daniele Verzini (color)
Graphics by Chiara Cebraro

Special thanks to Beth Dunfey
Translated by Emily Clement
Interior design by Kay Petronio

12 11 10 9 8 7 6 5 4 3 2 1   14 15 16 17 18 19/0

Printed in the U.S.A.   40
First printing, January 2014

A GIFT OF FLOWERS

The moment I opened the door to Flora Bloom's shop, a wave of delicious scents washed over me. The room was a whirl of color: hot-pink orchids, glowing yellow sunflowers, scarlet roses, milky-white lilies, WARM orange tulips. . . .

"Flora, there's no place on MOUSE ISLAND quite like your shop!" I exclaimed.

"Thank you, my dear Thea," she replied with a smile.

Oh, pardon me, I almost forgot to introduce myself! My name is THEA STILTON, and I am a special correspondent for *The Rodent's Gazette*, New Mouse City's biggest newspaper.

FLORA is an old friend.

"So what brings you here today?" Flora asked. "Oh, I know! You're here to —"

"— yes, to buy a big *bouquet* for Aunt Sweetfur's birthday!" I said. "You know how she *loves* flowers. I was thinking of an arrangement of lilies and irises. What do you think?"

Package? What package?

"That's a great **idea**. But actually, I thought you were here for the package that arrived this morning."

"**Package?** What package?" I asked, surprised. I wasn't expecting anything.

Flora disappeared into the back of the **store**. A moment later, she **EMERGED**

This!

carrying a small box. "This!" she **EXCLAIMED**, placing it on the counter. There was a **note** attached to one corner.

Dear Thea,
Please enjoy this souvenir of our latest amazing adventure. Care for it patiently, and you'll be rewarded with its beauty! You'll understand everything when you read the email we sent you with the complete tale of our trip.

Lots of love,
The Thea Sisters

I was more **CURIOUS** than a cat! You see, a while back, I'd returned to my old school, Mouseford Academy, to teach an adventure journalism class. Colette, nicky, PAMELA, PAULINA, and **Violet** — the THEA SISTERS — were my star students. I couldn't wait to see what they'd sent me.

I opened the package carefully. "It looks like . . . an onion?!"

Flora examined it, and then started to laugh. "It's not an onion, it's a tulip bulb."

A tulip? I immediately thought of the country that was famouse for those splendid flowers. Had the THEA SISTERS really been to **HOLLAND***? I scurried home to check my email. Soon I learned all about the fabumouse adventure I'm about to share with you, dear readers!

---

* Holland is a region of the Netherlands, and the name is often used to refer to the whole country.

FiVE miNUS ONE

The bell **RANG**, signaling the end of classes, and the students of Mouseford Academy scampered out of their classrooms in rowdy groups.

A butterfly!

Colette stopped for a moment to organize her *notes*. She was almost done when a huge **butterfly** flew in through an open window and landed next to her bag.

"Well, hello there. What are you doing in here?" the mouselet murmured. A *second* later, the butterfly headed back into the garden, where it landed on a flower that had just **bloomed**.

Colette glanced out the window and admired the wildflowers. SPRING had arrived all at once, like a sudden breath of fresh air.

"Colette, what are you still doing here? Aren't you coming to **lunch**?" asked Pam, poking her snout through the classroom door. "If we don't **hurry**, there won't be any free tables in the cafeteria."

"I've got a better idea!" Colette replied. "We don't need a table. Grab a blanket and let's go have a **picnic**. I want to enjoy this **GORGEOUS** spring day!"

Ten minutes later, the Thea Sisters were settling down under a tree in one corner of the garden.

"This was a **GREAT IDEA**, Colette!" Paulina

exclaimed. "Look at all these **MARVEMOUSE** flowers! I feel like we've stepped into a painting by Vincent van Gopher."

The mouselets exchanged a **look**. They were all thinking the same thing.

"I wonder how Violet's **PAINTING CLASS** is going," Nicky said.

"It's so amazing that she won that scholarship," Colette said.

"A month of study in the most famouse **STUDIO** in Amsterdam* is a dream come true for an art lover like her!" Paulina added.

"She'll definitely **learn** a lot," Pam said, nodding. "She probably already has. . . ."

The mouselets fell silent. It was as if the sky had **clouded** over their clear spring day.

"You know, I miss Violet a lot," sighed Colette, shaking her snout.

"Me, too!" **cried** Nicky.

* Amsterdam is the capital of the Netherlands.

Just then, they heard a familiar **SQUEAK** behind them. "There you are! I've been looking all over for you." Mercury Whale, Whale Island's mailmouse, scurried over to the mouselets.

"Really? Why, Mercury?" Pam asked.

Mercury started **RUMMAGING** through his big mailbag. Finally, he pulled out a large purple envelope. "Here, this is for you. It arrived this morning."

Here, this is for you.

"It's a letter from Violet!" Pam exclaimed. "Thanks, Mercury!"

The mouselets opened the ***envelope*** and settled down to read it.

MY LIFE IN HOLLAND

Dearest friends,

I hardly know how to begin! I have so many things to tell you that I'm afraid I'll forget something important.

I'm enclosing some photos and sketches that will give you an idea of everything I've been doing. I wanted to include some of the delicious *stroopwafels* they eat here, but they wouldn't fit in the envelope! (*Stroopwafels* are traditional cookies from Holland: two thin waffles with a layer of caramel between them.) Pam will have to settle for this drawing.

Okay, I'm getting ahead of myself! Let me back up and go in order.

My painting class with Professor de Wal keeps me very busy. From the moment I set paw in Amsterdam, I've spent most of my time in his studio. It's a truly magical place.

Every day, my fellow students and I take classes in art history, design, theory, and color technique. But the best part of the day is when we paint.

My classmates come from all over the world, and they're all very nice. I've become close friends with one of the local students, Jan van Garten. We share a love of music — he plays the violin, too!

Jan has showed me all his favorite spots in Amsterdam. We just came back from a tour of the city. We traveled across town in a crazy but cool way: on a tandem bicycle! In Amsterdam, bicycles are the most common way of getting around.

They're perfect for getting through

the streets in the center of the city, and for crossing the bridges that go over the canals.

It's wonderful to speed through the historic sections of Amsterdam. The sun glimmers through the trees, and the canals reflect the buildings and sky like mirrors.

Today we went to Dam Square, which is in the heart of the city. I was enjoying the sights so much that I was a little disappointed when Jan suggested that we stop for lunch. I didn't know that he wanted to take me to a special place: a fabumouse theater where we attended a classical music concert!

Later we had a picnic in the park, and Jan shared a local specialty with me: pickled herring. To be honest, it was a little strong for my taste, but I'll try anything once.

Jan has another adventure in store for me: In a few days, he'll take me to his father's greenhouse.

Casper van Garten is a famouse flower grower who specializes in tulips. He grows rare varieties and is always on the hunt for new hybrids. (A hybrid is a flower that is created by crossbreeding two kinds of flowers.) I'm sure Mr. Van Garten is a very kind rodent, just like his son. The cheese doesn't fall far from the cracker!

Thanks to Jan, I feel at home in Amsterdam, even though I miss you all very much. Not a single day

passes without my squeaking about you!
Jan says that he feels like he knows you
already.

I could keep writing for hours, but my
alarm goes off early in the morning, and

I don't want to be a sleepysnout at the studio tomorrow. (You know how grumpy I get when I'm drowsy!)

I'm enclosing a small painting that I made for you. I hope you like it!

Lots of hugs, and see you soon,
Violet

A FUNNY FEELING

As she **cleaned** her brushes at the end of painting class, Violet wondered if her **friends** had received her letter yet. She really missed seeing the other Thea Sisters every day.

Jan's *cheerful* squeak broke through her thoughts. "Hey, Violet, are you ready? We'd better haul tail. It takes at least twenty minutes to **walk** to my house."

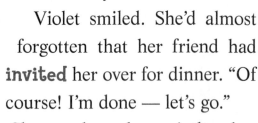

Violet smiled. She'd almost forgotten that her friend had **invited** her over for dinner. "Of course! I'm done — let's go."

She put down her paintbrushes and headed toward the **STUDIO** exit.

Jan chuckled. "Um, are you really planning to go out like that?"

"Yes, why?" Violet said. "I didn't get PAINT in my whiskers, did I?"

"No, your whiskers are clean. It's your clothes I'm concerned about!"

Violet looked down and started laughing: She hadn't realized that she was still wearing the PAINT-COVERED smock she'd put on for class. She quickly pulled it off and hung it up. "I'm ready now!"

Together the two friends plunged into the streets of Amsterdam.

"I think you'll have a nice time tonight," Jan promised his friend. "My father is more than just a tulip expert — he's also an excellent cook."

"I can't wait to taste some traditional Dutch food," Violet replied.

The SUNSET shone red on the surface of the canal they were crossing. Violet smiled.

It was so beautiful in Amsterdam!

A few minutes later, they **SPOTTED** Jan's house. "We're here!" he said. **WOOF! WOOF! WOOF!**

"That's Vincent, right?" exclaimed Violet at the sound of a dog **barking**. "I can't wait to meet him."

"Yes, but something's off. . . . He doesn't usually **bark** like that."

"Maybe he's **happy** to see you," Violet suggested. "Or maybe he knows that you have company."

As they drew closer to the house, though, they realized that Vincent was **RUNNING** back and forth in the yard.

"Strange. All the lights are out," Jan said, pointing at the house's windows. "Come on, let's go **INSIDE**. I have a funny feeling about this. . . ."

A DOUBLE DISAPPEARANCE

The moment he crossed through the door, Jan's funny feeling became a **certainty**. The house was empty.

"**PAPA?**" Jan called out as he entered the kitchen. He expected to find his father at the stove, but the room was dark and silent. The counter was covered with bags still filled with groceries. There was no TRACE of Casper anywhere.

There's no answer!

"Maybe he **remembered** one last ingredient and went out to get it," Violet suggested.

Jan called his **FATHER** on his cell phone, but there was no answer.

"Could he be in the **greenhouse**?" Violet asked.

"He doesn't usually go out there once it starts getting dark. But let's check," Jan said.

Outside, the sun had set, leaving the house shrouded in **DARKNESS**. The friends pushed open the greenhouse's door, hoping to **SEE** Jan's father.

The place was deserted. Violet walked between the blooming PLANTS that filled the greenhouse, calling out Casper's name, but no one responded.

"He's **DEFINITELY** not here. . . ." she murmured, discouraged.

"Oh no! It's . . . it's DISAPPEARED!" Jan cried.

"I'm sure he hasn't DISAPPEARED. He must have gone out for some reason," Violet reassured her friend.

"Not my father," her friend replied. "The

TULIP BULB is gone!"

"What tulip bulb?"

Jan pointed to an empty shelf. "The **HYBRID** my father created! It's a bulb he invented by **crossing** many kinds of tulips. He's been working on it for months. It used to be on this shelf, and now it's GONE!"

Violet frowned. "Could he have moved it or taken it away for some reason?"

TULIPS THROUGH THE CENTURIES

Tulips were imported to the Netherlands from Turkey during the second half of the sixteenth century. Residents of Holland soon became major tulip cultivators and merchants.

There are more than a hundred known species of tulips, and new **hybrids** are being created all the time. Botanists cross many different kinds of tulips to produce unique colors and characteristics.

The ratlet shook his snout. "There was no **reason** to move it. It was there because he needed to watch it and take care of it. He was planning to present it to the DUTCH BOTANIC COMMITTEE the day after tomorrow."

"That's strange . . . and a little suspicious," said Violet. "But we shouldn't jump to **conclusions**. There might be a simple explanation for the **DISAPPEARANCE** of the bulb — and your father."

Jan shook his snout again. "My father isn't the kind of mouse to vanish like this. And the fact that his valuable **tulip** bulb is missing, too . . ." Jan's squeak trailed off. "Something happened to him. I just know it!"

"What do you mean?" Violet asked.

"There are rodents who will do anything to get their paws on something rare like this.

They could have swiped the bulb . . . and done something **BAD** to my father!"

Violet looked at her friend's worried snout. She knew exactly what to do.

"Don't worry, Jan. We need help, and I know how to get it. Come on, I have to make a phone call." With that, she took Jan by the paw and **pulled** him out of the greenhouse.

REINFORCEMENTS ARE HERE!

At the airport in **AMSTERDAM**, a group of four mouselets was **STRUGGLING** to make their way through the crowd.

"Relax, Colette, the lost luggage desk is right there," Paulina said, **pointing** to a window a short distance away.

"I can't believe they lost my favorite **LITTLE** bag." Colette sighed.

"**LITTLE** bag?!" Pam snorted. "As usual, you brought your entire **wardrobe** with you."

"Pam, I thought we went over this already," Colette replied. "What is **Holland** famouse for?"

"Um . . . its cheese?"

"No, its WINDMILLS! And where there are lots of windmills, there's lots of —"

"**FLOUR!**" Pam exclaimed. "That means bread, cakes, and pizza . . . yum!"

"Not flour, *wind*!" Colette cried, rolling her eyes. "There's lots of wind! And too much wind is terrible for your fur. So I absolutely needed my MOISTURIZING KIT. It's only twelve little bottles. Plus a few hats."

"A *few*?" Pam tried to stifle a GIGGLE.

A few?!

Okay, maybe more than a few!

"There were at least a dozen!"

While the two friends **BICKERED**, Nicky and Paulina went up to the counter and asked for information.

"Colette?" Paulina said a moment later, **tapping** her friend on the shoulder. "We know what happened to your SUITCASE."

"Really?" asked Colette, whirling around. "Did they find it?"

"Well, we never lost it, miss," a customer service representative replied politely. "It's over there."

The mouselets **TURNED** around. A porter was struggling to push Colette's **ENORMOUSE** pink suitcase, which had been labeled OVERSIZED BAGGAGE.

Colette blushed **redder** than a tomato. Her friends burst out laughing.

"There's your little bag!" Pam teased.

Colette's ears DROOPED with embarrassment. But it didn't last long. Once the mouselets had boarded the TRAIN that would take them to the Amsterdam city center, she perked up again.

"What do you think the emergency is?" she asked. "It's not like Violet to bring us here in such a rush."

"I was just thinking about that," Nicky said. "On the phone she mentioned the disappearance of a precious tulip bulb."

"She seemed really worried," Paulina agreed. "Well, soon we'll all be together and she can tell us the whole STORY."

THE FIRST CLUE

An hour later, Colette, Nicky, Pam, and Paulina had reached Jan's house. The sight of Violet made them **HAPPIER** than a pack of hungry mouselings in an overstocked cheese pantry. There was a quick round of hugs.

Violet immediately introduced Jan to her friends.

He filled the mouselets in on the details of his father's DISAPPEARANCE the previous evening — and on the disappearance of his father's precious botanical **experiment**, a new tulip hybrid.

"I can't stay here and wait for my father to return," said Jan. "I have to DO something! I think he's in **DANGER**."

Violet placed a comforting paw on her friend's shoulder. "Let's THINK about this. We need to find out what your father did yesterday."

"That's right, we should reconstruct his movements," Paulina agreed. "Where's his **COMPUTER**? He might have some appointments in his calendar."

A smile flickered across Jan's snout. "Not on his computer. You have to understand, my father is a very **old-fashioned** mouse.

He prefers to use an old paper *planner*."
He began rummaging through a desk drawer.
"I think he keeps it in here. . . ."

A moment later, Jan placed a cloth-covered
notebook on the kitchen table. He flipped it
open to the day of the disappearance.

"**Flower auction?**" Pam asked.
"What does that mean?"

"It's an important event for rodents who
buy and sell flowers,"
Jan explained. "At
Aalsmeer*, you can
find the **most**
SOUGHT-AFTER kinds
of flowers. My
father goes there
all the time."

"There's another
note below that —

April 24
- Call the dentist
- Flower auction at
Aalsmeer

Remember the
BLACK TULIP

---

* Aalsmeer is a small town in Holland that is home to
an important flower market.

'Remember the **BLACK TULIP**.' Is that a special kind of flower?" Paulina asked.

"Actually, *The Black Tulip* is the name of a famouse NOVEL," said Violet.

"That's right!" Jan said. "It's my father's favorite book. He recently talked about having his antique edition rebound. That's probably what he's referring to here."

"Okay. It sounds like we should begin our iNVeStiGatiON in Aalsmeer," Pam declared.

"All right, then, let's move our tails!" said Colette.

THE BLACK TULIP

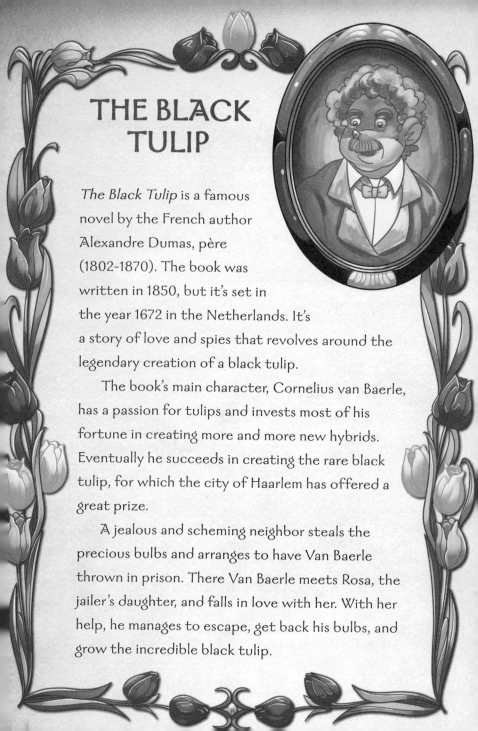

The Black Tulip is a famous novel by the French author Alexandre Dumas, père (1802-1870). The book was written in 1850, but it's set in the year 1672 in the Netherlands. It's a story of love and spies that revolves around the legendary creation of a black tulip.

The book's main character, Cornelius van Baerle, has a passion for tulips and invests most of his fortune in creating more and more new hybrids. Eventually he succeeds in creating the rare black tulip, for which the city of Haarlem has offered a great prize.

A jealous and scheming neighbor steals the precious bulbs and arranges to have Van Baerle thrown in prison. There Van Baerle meets Rosa, the jailer's daughter, and falls in love with her. With her help, he manages to escape, get back his bulbs, and grow the incredible black tulip.

THE FLOWER AUCTION

The mouselets and Jan hurried to catch a **BUS** to Aalsmeer.

"Have you been to the *flower auction* before?" Violet asked.

"Yes, my father has taken me many times. A **GOOD FRIEND** of his, Hendrik, works there."

"Oh, that's great. We can ask him if he **SAW** your father yesterday — and if he noticed anything **unusual**," said Paulina.

Jan nodded **solemnly**. He looked gloomier than a groundhog who'd just seen his shadow.

Violet took his **paw** in her own. "We'll **find** your father, you'll see."

"We're not leaving here without helping you get to the **BOTTOM** of this," Colette

declared. "THEA SISTERS' HONOR!"

Jan gave the mouselets a warm smile. "NOW I understand why Violet squeaks so often about you. You are **true and loyal** friends!"

Just then, the bus stopped.

"Follow me, and stay close. This place is so big that it's easy to get lost," Jan said. He led the mouselets off the bus and into the home of the world's largest *flower auction*.

The mouselets' **EYES** widened at the sight of thousands of colorful boxes filled with flowers of every kind.

"Whoa, this place is **ENORMOUSE**!" exclaimed Pam. "Jan, I'm sticking to you closer than a glue trap."

"It's amazing! I've never seen so many 𝒻𝓁𝑜𝓌𝑒𝓇𝓈 all in one place!" cried Paulina.

"The auction is almost over," Jan explained. "They're preparing the shipments to be sent all over the world. . . . **LOOK!**"

The mouselets saw rodents pushing multicolored carts through the aisles.

"How are we going to spot Hendrik in all this **CONFUSION**?" Pam asked.

"I know where to **FIND** him. Follow me!" Jan led the mouselets to the ꜱhipping area. A rodent wearing a red cap was loading a **BOX** of small pink tulips onto a cart.

"Hendrik!" Jan called out.

The rodent turned and **beamed**. "Jan, my dear ratlet! It's been a while since we've seen you around here. How are you?"

"I'm fine, thank you, although unfortunately this is **not** just a friendly visit. . . ."

THE FLOWER AUCTION AT AALSMEER

The village of AALSMEER, about eight miles southwest of Amsterdam, is home to the largest flower market in all of Europe. Every day, thousands of flowers and plants are bought and sold at AUCTION. In addition to classic tulips, which are a symbol of Holland, buyers can purchase flowers from all over the world.

A few large monitors display what's happening in the auction, indicating the PRICE, the KIND of flower, and the QUANTITY. As the day goes on, the price gets lower, not higher. Over fifty million plants and flowers are sold each day.

A flower warehouse in Aalsmeer with boxes of flowers stacked up

This is the hall where the flower auction takes place, with large monitors and a catwalk where you can watch the action.

"What do you mean?" asked Hendrik.

"I'm **LOOKING** for my father: I haven't heard anything from him since yesterday, and I know he came through here. These are my **friends** Violet, Colette, Nicky, Pam, and Paulina. They're helping me."

"Now that I **think** about it, I saw your father yesterday. He was not far from here," said Hendrik. "He was talking to a female rodent I'd never seen **before**."

"Can you describe her?" Violet asked.

Hendrik nodded. "She was tall, with **LONG red FUR**, and she was dressed very elegantly. She and Casper were so

absorbed in their conversation I didn't want to INTERRUPT them."

Paulina made notes on her MousePad. "Tall, red fur, elegant . . . that's not much to go on for **identification**. Can you remember anything else?"

The rodent **closed** his eyes in **concentration**. "Hmm, let's see . . . well, I heard them mention the LILAC PAGODA. . . ."

"What's that?" Pam asked.

Hendrik shook his snout. "Unfortunately, I have no idea!"

Casper was seen talking to a mysterious female rodent. Who could she be? And what is the Lilac Pagoda?

THE MYSTERIOUS LILAC PAGODA

The Thea Sisters **EXCHANGED** glances.

"We need to learn more about this LILAC PAGODA," Violet said. "It could lead us to the rodent who was squeaking with Casper."

"Paulina, you have a **floor plan**, right?" Colette asked. "Maybe the Lilac Pagoda is here somewhere."

The mouselets consulted the floor plan, but there was no place in the flower market with that name.

"Let's split up and look for **CLUES**," Paulina suggested. "If we ask around, I'm sure we'll learn something."

Unfortunately, after a full half hour of

exploration, the Thea Sisters failed to turn up any helpful **information**.

Jan was getting discouraged. "Time is passing and there's still no sign of my father. I don't know what to do!"

Hendrik put a paw on his shoulder. "Your **father** is a smart rodent. He can handle any situation. Don't worry!"

"Hendrik is right," Violet said. "We can't lose hope. Let's think about our next step."

"Why don't we sit down and talk it out?" Paulina proposed. "Let's go to a little café that Nicky and I PASSED earlier."

"I'll come with you. I want to help you find Casper," Hendrik declared.

A few **MOMENTS** later, Hendrik, Jan, and the mouselets were seated at a big table, sipping **cool** drinks.

"Okay, so we know that Casper came here

yesterday and squeaked with a mysterious rodent with **RED FUR**," Violet began.

"He probably had an appointment with her," Hendrik said. "I got the sense that they **KNEW** each other."

"How about a little snack while we talk?" suggested Pam. "My stomach's **rumbling** louder than a souped-up sports car."

"Pam, you never change," Nicky said, **LAUGHING**.

Let's review!

"I don't think well on an empty stomach. It's like trying to start an **SUV** without gas!" her friend explained.

The mouselets ordered a cheese plate. "SIZZLING SPARK PLUGS, this looks **GREAT**," Pam exclaimed. "Yum! Now, that's what I call **BRAIN FOOD!**"

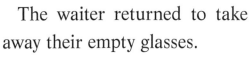

The waiter returned to take away their empty glasses.

"If only we knew where to find the LILAC PAGODA . . ." Colette sighed.

"The *Lilac Pagoda*?" the waiter said. "Pardon me for **interrupting**, but it's just a short walk from here."

The mouselets **LOOKED** at him, their snouts hanging open in surprise. "You know where it is? Can you show us what street it's on?"

The ratlet laughed. "It's not on a street. I saw it this morning — it's **docked** at the lake."

"Docked? But that means . . . it's a boat!" Colette said.

"**Of course**," the waiter replied. "A really spectacular one, too."

Jan threw down some money to pay the bill. He, Hendrik, and the **mouselets** headed toward the exit. Only Pam stayed behind to finish the last few bites of **cheese**.

It's a spectacular boat!

"Come on, Pam!" Violet urged her.

"**Yes . . . yum . . . I'm coming!**" her friend replied, scurrying after them. "Sorry, but my motto is 'leave no cheese behind'!"

CHASE ON THE CANAL

Hendrik led the group to the lake's edge. "Come on, the dock the waiter pointed out is this way!"

Their search wasn't DIFFICULT. As soon as they turned the corner, the Thea Sisters spotted a magnificent **purple boat** with brass trim that gleamed in the sunlight. On the keel, the words LILAC PAGODA were spelled out in elegant script.

"We found it!" Violet exclaimed.

Nicky dashed toward the boat. She'd seen the shape of a female rodent ON BOARD, and a **FLASH** of red fur lit by the sun. It must be the mouse they were looking for!

Nicky tried to call out to her, but the rodent

quickly went into the cabin. That's when Nicky noticed the image of a large **BLACK TULIP** on the back of the boat.

A moment later, the boat's engine started.

"What's happening?" Paulina asked Nicky when she and the others caught up.

"We found her," Nicky replied, "but she's **GETTING AWAY**!"

"Oh no! Now how will we follow her?" Paulina exclaimed.

"I have a **solution**, mouselets," Hendrik said. "Her name is *ANNABEL*!"

The Thea Sisters exchanged a confused

look. "Is Annabel the red-furred rodent? Do you know her?"

"*Annabel* isn't a rodent — she's Hendrik's boat," Jan explained.

Hendrik nodded. "Come with me. She's docked right over here."

A few moments later, the Thea Sisters and their friends were zooming through the lake's peaceful waters, following the mysterious rodent's lilac boat.

"I think she spotted us. She's speeding up!" Violet cried in dismay.

"You're right!" Hendrik called from the wheel of the *ANNABEL*. He put his paw on the gas.

"What is she RUNNING away from?" Pam asked.

When the Thea Sisters call out to the mysterious rodent, she doesn't respond, and then she flees. Why? Is she hiding something?

"She must have something to hide. . . ." said Violet suspiciously.

"But what? We've got to catch up to her so we can find out!" Nicky said.

"We've almost reached the other side of the lake, but the LILAC PAGODA hasn't slowed down," Colette said in alarm.

"It's taking a **CANAL**," Jan explained. "Holland has an extensive canal system. We can use it to make our way out of the city."

While Hendrik steered the boat toward the canal, the mouselets kept their eyes on the strange BOAT. After a few minutes, they saw it pull up to a small dock. The female rodent scrambled off the boat and rushed away.

It took several minutes for the *Annabel* to reach the **dock** and for the Thea Sisters and Jan to disembark.

"We're in Lisse*," Hendrik said as he helped them off the boat. "Unfortunately, I can't stay with you any longer. I must return to the flower market. But please keep me updated!"

Jan nodded. "Thanks, Hendrik. We hope to send you good news soon."

* Lisse is a town in Holland about seventeen miles southwest of Amsterdam. It's famous for the Keukenhof botanic garden.

THE ELUSIVE RODENT

The rodent with **Reᴅ Fuʀ** seemed to have eluded her pursuers. Once they had set paw on dry **LAND**, they didn't know where to start looking.

"We could try asking passersby," Colette suggested. "With that bright red fur, she certainly isn't the kind of rodent who could pass UNNOTICED."

Pam stopped a ratlet on a skateboard. "Excuse me, have you seen an elegant rodent with red fur?"

"Yes, she rushed past me — I had to be careful not to *run over* her. She went that way," the ratlet replied, pointing in the direction away from the canal.

She went that way!

After him, an elderly rodent directed the friends toward the MYSTERIOUS rodent.

"It looks like she's heading to Keukenhof*, the flower park," Jan exclaimed. "If she went in there, it won't be **easy** to find her."

"Why?" Paulina asked. But as soon as she and her friends laid **EYES** on Keukenhof, they understood. The park was filled with fragrant plants and FLOWERS, and it was enormouse!

"It's so beautiful," Paulina said, admiring the flower beds of tulips, narcissus, and daffodils.

"It's gorgeous, right?" Jan said with a smile. "It's one of PAPA'S favorite places."

---

* Keukenhof is the largest bulb park in the world. It has over one hundred varieties of tulip!

The thought of his father made a shadow pass over Jan's snout. But just then, Violet spotted red fur in the distance. "There she is!" she exclaimed.

The group resumed their chase, but once again, the rodent managed to escape them.

"Where did she go?!" Jan cried in confusion.

"I don't know. Let's split up!" Nicky said, running down a path.

"Wait! There she is!" Pam exclaimed as she approached a COPPER-FURRED rodent whose back was to her.

"Excuse me, ma'am! Stop! Why are you running away?" Pam asked her.

"Running away?" the rodent replied, turning to Pam. "What do you mean?"

Pam took a step back and turned bright red. This wasn't the rodent they'd seen on the

boat! She was just a rodent with red fur.

"Um . . . I'm sorry, I **MiSTOOK** you for someone else. . . ." Pam said, returning to her friends with her snout down.

"Mouselets, I can't believe I'm squeaking this, but it looks like we've been following the **WRONG** strand of string cheese!" she concluded sadly.

A NEW STRATEGY

The mouselets looked at one another, feeling more **LOST** than lab rats in a maze.

"Now what do we do?" Violet asked. "We'll never find her!"

"Keep calm and carry on, sisters!" Colette exclaimed. "Let's review the situation and FORMULATE a plan."

Jan checked his watch *nervously*. "Mouselets, I think the best thing to do is return to Amsterdam and report my father's disappearance to the police. He's been missing for a whole day!"

"You're right," Paulina said, "but we can't ABANDON the chase yet! The mysterious rodent can't have gone far."

"Then I'll go back to Amsterdam while

you continue the search," Jan suggested. "This **EVENING** my father was going to present the bulb he created to the DUTCH BOTANIC COMMITTEE. He's been preparing for this meeting for months."

"What are you planning to do?" Pam asked. "The bulb is gone, too."

"If my father doesn't get back in time, I'll go to the meeting, explain the situation, and ask for more time," Jan said, shrugging.

It's getting late! I'm going back to Amsterdam.

"I'm coming with you," said Violet.

"Yes, you shouldn't be alone," Paulina said kindly.

"We'll stay HERE. I know

we'll find something," Nicky declared.

"Okay," Violet replied. "The first ones to find **news** about Casper will let the others know."

The mouselets said good-bye, and Jan and Violet headed toward the park's **EXIT**.

"Sisters, look! I think I've found a way for us to search the area," said Pam, pointing to a kiosk labeled BIKES AND TANDEMS FOR RENT.

"You're a **genius**, Pam!" Nicky replied,

BIKES AND TANDEMS FOR RENT

heading in that direction.

The mouselets **followed** her to the kiosk, and a moment later they left on two bicycles and a **taNDeM**.

"Where to next?" Pam asked.

"Let's split up into two groups. Pam, you and I will go **tHat Way**," Colette replied, pointing to a path that led into a thick group of trees.

"Paulina and I will head toward that **windmill**," Nicky said, pointing in the opposite direction.

With that, the mouselets headed off in search of **CLUES**.

THE BLACK TULIP

Paulina and Nicky **RACED** along a path bordered by thousands of brightly colored tulips.

"Slow down!" Paulina shouted to her friend. They were together on the tandem, and Nicky was pedaling *faster* than a hyperactive hamster on a wheel.

"What's wrong, Paulina? Eat too many **cheese puffs** for breakfast this morning?" she asked teasingly.

"No, you're just going way too fast! If we speed along, we won't **SEE** the mysterious rodent go past, even if she's right under the tips of our snouts!"

"That's true. . . ." her friend admitted, and slowed her pace.

The two continued along, **carefully** scrutinizing every snout in every corner of the **PARK**. But they didn't find a trace of the mysterious rodent.

Meanwhile, Pam and Colette were cycling through the park, too, with no more success than their friends.

"Colette, why do you think the **MYSTERIOUS** rodent keeps scurrying away from us?" Pam asked.

"I have no idea, but I'm sure it has something to do with Casper's **disappearance**. That's why we've got to find her!"

As they chatted, the two mouselets **exited** the park. They reached a

street that ran along a canal on one side and was bordered by WOODS on the other.

Pam and Colette hopped off their BIKES to rest their paws for a moment. That's when Pam spotted a wall hidden behind the bushes.

"What's that?" she wondered.

"Did you FIND something?" asked Colette.

"Look! There's a sign!" Pam exclaimed, pointing to a plaque peeking out from behind the vines.

"Hey, that symbol is the same one we saw on the mysterious rodent's boat!" Colette observed. "Let's check it out."

The two friends made their way along the wall. Soon they came to a gate that was locked up TIGHT. The decorations on the gate formed the shape of a TULIP.

"The black tulip!" Pam exclaimed.

The mouselets peered beyond the gate. Not far away, they could make out a SQUARE building with dark green walls. Through one of the first-floor windows they saw the shape of a rodent with long red fur.

"Did you see that?" Colette whispered. "It must be her!"

"Let's call the others," said Nicky. "It looks like we're finally sniffing after the right hunk of cheese!"

Colette and Pam found a gate marked with the same black tulip that was painted on the boat belonging to the rodent with red fur. What could it mean?

A REVEALING DETAIL

Back in **Amsterdam**, Violet and Jan were scampering back from the bus station. As soon as they **passed** through the gate to Jan's house, a floppy mound of fur launched itself at the ratlet, knocking him to the ground.

"Vincent!" Jan cried to his dog. "Poor boy, you've been **ALONE** all this time."

"He can't wait to **PLAY** with you!" Violet said, laughing.

"And to **crunch** on something tasty," Jan replied. "It's been hours since he's eaten. Let's go **feed** him."

The two friends

Vincent!

went into the house. Everything was just as they'd left it that morning. There was still no TRACE of Casper.

Jan took a can of dog food out of the PANTRY. "My father was supposed to present the BULB tonight at eight o'clock," he told Violet.

"It's too bad there's nothing

How lovely!

you can show the committee," she replied.

"It is. I wish I knew who could have gotten their paws on my father's **precious creation**," Jan said, putting the food in Vincent's bowl.

The dog **WAGGED** his tail happily. He was following Jan's every movement. A little **drool** dripped from his jaws as he waited for his food.

"Jan, **HOW LOVELY**! Is this your Van Gopher **reproduction**?" Violet asked, admiring a painting hanging on a wall.

"Yes, it's one of the first things I painted at the **STUDIO**," Jan replied.

Jan was so distracted, he didn't notice Vincent's hungry **yelps** when he left the food dish on the kitchen counter. "That's the famous painting *Bedroom in Arles* — you

Can you tell the difference between the original and Jan's reproduction?

know, the R O O M where Vincent van Gopher lived. When my father saw it, he was convinced that I had a real *talent* for painting, and he wanted to hang it up."

"It's really well done, Jan. Your father was right," Violet said.

"You should have seen how *proud* he was," Jan said. "You know, he studied painting when he was **YOUNG**, too, but he stopped because it wasn't for him. He's always said that he preferred to 'produce art on the petals of TULIPS'! And so — *hey!*"

The ratlet suddenly interrupted himself. "Look! There's something new here . . . and I didn't paint it!"

Violet LOOKED more closely at the painting. "Of course — the **tulip**!" she said. "In the original painting, there's nothing in the vase."

"Exactly!" Jan confirmed, studying the new detail.

"Are you sure you didn't PAINT that?" Violet asked.

"POSITIVE!" he said.

Violet was confused. "WHO could have done it? And what does it mean?"

"I think I know who it was: my father!" Jan cried. "I recognize his beginner's stroke. Plus, the yellow-and-pink tulip is the same hybrid variety that he's been working on."

"Then it must be a CLUE!" Violet exclaimed. "Now we just need to figure out what the hidden message is. . . ."

Why did Casper add a tulip to Jan's painting?

A MATTER OF PERSPECTIVE

Jan started to pace **BACK** and *FORTH* like a cat outside a mousehole. Still hoping for his dinner, Vincent followed his every movement.

"Why would my FATHER add a tulip to the painting?" Jan wondered.

"Hmm, let's think about it," said Violet. "Okay, so we have a **missing** bulb, and a TULIP has suddenly appeared on the canvas. . . . I've got it! The tulip will lead us to the **BULB**!"

"That's BRILLIANT, Violet!" Jan said, beaming.

"My father probably felt **threatened** by someone who wanted to steal his creation.

So he **LEFT** a clue only I would be able to figure out. . . ."

The enthusiasm on the ratlet's snout was suddenly replaced with disappointment. "Except that I can't make snouts or tails of it!"

"We could find the other **Van Gopher PAINTINGS** you've reproduced," Violet suggested. "Where do you keep them?"

"In my room. Come on!"

The two friends searched Jan's room, and

then all over the house, for Casper's **bulb**, but they didn't find anything.

"This is **HARDER** than finding a cheese slice in a haystack," Jan sighed. "It's no use! We've **combed** through the whole house."

He was interrupted by a sudden racket down in the kitchen. Jan and Violet rushed downstairs. The scene before them left them squeakless.

Vincent had jumped onto the kitchen counter to get his food dish. But he was clumsier than a raccoon in a rubbish bin, and he'd **pushed** it off the counter, **along** with some plates that were stacked nearby.

"Vincent!" Jan scolded him. Then he suddenly stopped and turned to his friend. *"Vincent's room . . ."* he murmured.

"That's it! You figured out what the clue means!" Violet exclaimed.

"Our Vincent's **ROOM**," Jan continued. "Which is . . ."

". . . **the doghouse!**" Violet concluded.

The two *rushed* into the garden where, not far from the greenhouse, they found the large **WOODEN** doghouse that belonged to Vincent.

Jan crouched down to **look** inside. A moment later, he exclaimed, "**There it is!**"

When he stood up again, he was holding a small box. He placed it carefully in his friend's paws.

"The tulip **bulb** . . ." she whispered as Jan pulled it out of the box. "We found it!"

MADAME LILIA . . .
C'EST MOI!*

Back in Lisse, Colette, Nicky, Pam, and Paulina had gathered in front of the **mysterious** building, trying to figure out what to do.

"Hmm . . . We could walk around the building and see if the **WALL** continues on all sides," Nicky proposed.

"Or we could wait until someone comes out," Pam suggested. "If we're **lucky**, we'll run right into our rodent."

Colette was doubtful. "No, maybe it would be better to —"

"**I've got it!**" Paulina suddenly exclaimed. "Come look!"

She showed her **friends** her MousePad.

* *"Madame Lilia . . . c'est moi!"* means "Mrs. Lilac . . . that's me!" in French.

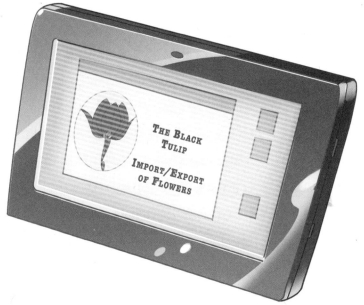

"The black tulip is the symbol and the name of a company that **deals** in flowers," Paulina explained. "However, there's VERY LITTLE information available about them online."

"The company is only a few months old, and I don't see the name of the owner **anywhere**," Pam commented, studying the screen carefully.

"But the rarest **tulips** are included on their product list. . . ."

"So they could be connected to Casper's research!" Nicky exclaimed.

Only Colette didn't JOIN the discussion among her friends. She hung back with an intense look of concentration on her snout.

Pam noticed. "Colette, is something wrong?"

"Nope, not at all! I think I've figured it all out!" Colette replied.

I've figured it out!

"Figured what out?"

"Do you remember the appointment on Casper's **calendar** that said 'BLACK TULIP'? We thought he was referring to a **book**, but . . ."

"He was talking about this company!" Paulina **GUESSED**. "What if Casper had an appointment with the mysterious rodent with ⦿⦿⦿ ⦿⦿⦿?"

"Do you **THINK** there's something suspicious going on inside?" Pam asked. "Maybe Casper trusted this unknown rodent, believing that she was honest . . . and instead she betrayed him somehow?"

The mouselets exchanged a **worried** look.

"We must go inside and squeak to the owner," Nicky declared.

"I have the solution in my purse," Colette exclaimed. "Here!"

"A hat and sunglasses? We're not going to the beach, Colette," Pam said.

Colette **smiled**. "I know that! But these are the perfect accessories for a disguise. . . ."

The mouselet put on the sunglasses and

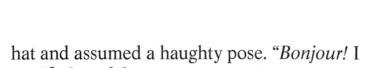

hat and assumed a haughty pose. *"Bonjour!* I am **Madame Lilia**!"

"Colette, I think the cheese has finally slipped off your cracker," Pam said. "Who the heck is Madame Lilia?"

Bonjour!

"A **rich** buyer of precious bulbs, here from France to purchase ƒℓowers from the Black Tulip!"

Seeing the squeakless looks on her friends' snouts, she explained, "I'll pretend to be a flower buyer and ask for a **meeting** with the owner of the company. Then I'll finally get to meet our mysterious rodent!"

"Great **idea**, Colette!" Paulina said.

LET'S REVIEW THE SITUATION!

- Jan's father, Casper, has mysteriously disappeared, and his precious tulip bulb disappeared with him!

- Before he disappeared, Casper left his son a clue that revealed the bulb's hiding place. Maybe he knew he was in danger.

- In his calendar, Casper had jotted down two appointments for the day he disappeared: the auction at Aalsmeer and a meeting with the Black Tulip.

- At Aalsmeer, Casper was seen talking to a mysterious rodent with red fur.

- The Thea Sisters tried to squeak with the mysterious rodent, but she ran away.

- The red-furred rodent got on a boat with a black tulip symbol on it — the same symbol on the gate at the mysterious building Pam and Colette just discovered.

A DARING IDEA

Colette's **strategy** worked. She pressed the intercom and introduced herself as a buyer, and the gate OPENED immediately. Nicky, Pam, and Paulina took the **opportunity** to SLIP through the gate and hide in the bushes just outside the building while they waited for their friend to complete her MISSION. Meanwhile, Colette had reached the doorstep, where a butler was waiting to take her straight to the OFFICE. They walked down an ENDLESS

This way, please.

marble hallway, which opened into a large room with dark walls.

The butler asked her to make herself **comfortable**, explaining, "**Verbena** will see you shortly."

Colette looked around, hoping for clues, but the room was bare. Suddenly, a door she hadn't noticed opened in the wall in front of her, and a rodent with **RED FUR** entered the room.

Colette was struck squeakless: The rodent that stood before her wasn't the same one they'd FOLLOWED on the boat! Verbena had red fur, but she was wearing **glasses** and a purple pantsuit, not a purple **SKIRT** and jacket like the rodent they'd seen earlier.

"Please **FOLLOW** me," Verbena said, leading Colette to her office.

"So, are you here on behalf of a company,

Madame Lilia?" she asked.

"Um, no, I'm a private buyer. I grow the rarest varieties in my garden," Colette replied. She carefully listed the names of several **floral** varieties that she'd noticed on flower labels in Keukenhof.

Verbena nodded and asked her to sit. "You've come to the right place. Here we have varieties for all tastes . . . and for all **PRICES**," she commented with an eager sparkle in her eyes. "Are you interested in anything in particular?"

"You don't happen to have a new type of bulb? For example, a tulip hybrid?" Colette asked.

"Of course. We have **MANY**," Verbena replied impatiently.

"Yes, but the usual tulips bore me. I need something unique! I heard that the famouse botanist Van Garten was working on a new **HYBRID**. Do you know anything about that?"

Verbena was startled. "I don't see why I should know this Van Garten. . . ." she said suspiciously.

"But I was told to talk to the rodents at **THE BLACK TULIP. . . .**"

"I've never heard of him, I'm sorry. It seems we can't help you. And now I should return to my **WORK**," Verbena said. She stood up abruptly and walked Colette to the door.

"But, wait —"

"**Good-bye**," the red-furred rodent concluded coldly, pushing Colette toward the door.

A **moment** later, Colette was back in the hallway. The butler appeared out of nowhere, escorted her to the exit in $silence$, and

CLUE!

Good-bye!

THE BLACK TULIP

Did you notice what's on the table? Why did Verbena freeze as soon as Colette mentioned Jan's father?

closed the door behind her.

"Pssst, Colette, we're over here!" Pam whispered from behind a thick bush.

Colette checked to make sure no one was looking, and then rejoined her friends.

"Well?" Nicky asked curiously.

"I met a rodent with RED FUR. Her name is Verbena," Colette confided. "She *looks* like the rodent we followed in the boat, but she isn't the same mouse. And she didn't tell me anything useful."

"Then this is a dead end?!" asked Paulina.

"Oh, I wouldn't say that! As I was leaving her office, I spotted an important CLUE: There was a book on her

Pssst! We're here!

table. And guess what the title was: THE BLACK TULIP!"

"Well, it's also the name of the business," said Nicky. "Maybe Verbena just likes that book. . . ."

"Not so fast, Nick! Inside the **book** was a bookmark engraved with three initials: CVG."

"Casper van Garten," Paulina breathed. "Jan's father!"

"What's his **book** doing here?" Pam asked.

"That's what we need to find out," Colette declared.

A DANGEROUS PLAN

The **path** before the mouselets was clear: They had to sneak into the Black Tulip offices and look for more **CLUES**.

"But how are we going to get back in?" Pam asked.

"**Madame Lilia** to the rescue!" Colette replied.

She sketched out her plan in her notebook. When Colette rang the doorbell again, she said that she'd forgotten her **sunglasses** case. Grumbling, the butler let her in.

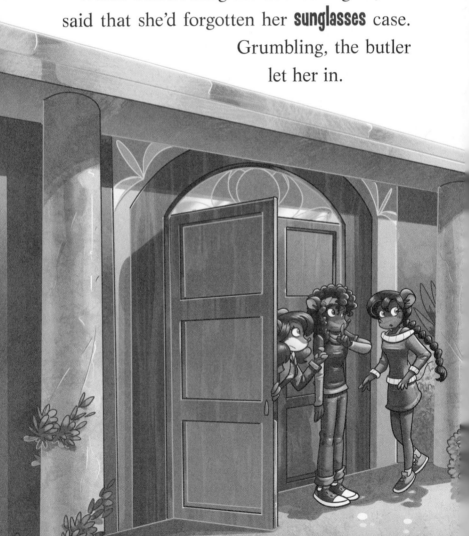

While Colette distracted him with some idle chatter, the others **SNEAKED** into the building and hid in a little room off the main hall.

"How is Colette going to **fit** through this tiny space?!" Pam said, forcing open the room's only window.

"No worries, Pam. Colette is very resourceful!" Nicky snickered.

Soon, their friend squeezed through the

What do you need? I forgot something!

window into the room, moaning, "What a cat-astrophe!"

"What is it? Trouble with the butler? Did he see you?!" Paulina asked.

Colette shook her snout. "No. But when I climbed up here, I chipped my paw polish!"

"Colette, when you're making a cheesecake, sometimes you've gotta break a few eggs," Nicky said, smiling. "Okay, where do we start?"

"When I followed Verbena to her office," Colette murmured, "I saw a room that looked like a laboratory. We could start there."

The mouselets cautiously stuck their snouts out into the hallway.

"ALL CLEAR!" Pam whispered.

Colette started to lead her friends toward the laboratory, but then Paulina grabbed her by the paw.

"What's wrong? We need to hurry. . . ."

"LISTEN!"

They all strained their ears to listen: the unmistakable tap-tap-tap of high heels was coming closer.

"**Verbena**! She's coming this way! Hide!" spluttered Pam, **squeezing** into a tiny closet.

The other THEA SISTERS, caught by surprise, **scurried** toward the lab and ducked inside.

A CHASE IN THE DARK

Verbena strode down the hallway that the Thea Sisters had just **HURRIED THROUGH**. She was talking on her **cell phone**. She stopped suddenly in front of a painting.

Pam chewed her WHISKERS nervously behind the almost-closed closet door. As long as the red-furred rodent stayed outside, she was trapped!

"Are you on your way? Great," Pam heard her say. "See you in five minutes."

Huddled in the closet, Pam realized she was surrounded by mops and work clothes. A brilliant idea came to her: If she disguised herself as a janitor, she could explore the building UNNOTICED. It was the perfect way to **LOOK** for clues!

She slipped into a jumpsuit and slapped a **CAP** on her head. Then she peeked out and saw that Verbena had DISAPPEARED.

Pam was just leaving her hiding place when she heard pawsteps in the distance. Another rodent with RED FUR was walking down the hallway. Pam crept out of the supply closet and followed her.

The rodent headed toward a door at the end of the HALLWAY and threw it open. It led to a large, brightly lit room, where Pam saw Verbena seated at a desk.

The other rodent went in and closed the door behind her.

Pam inched closer to the door and started to PUSH a mop around in the hallway, as if she were really cleaning. She listened intently.

"Today a French buyer came by. . . . I don't REMEMBER her name. I had never HEARD it before," Verbena was saying. "She asked me about Casper van

Garten's !"

"Really? What a strange coincidence," the other replied.

"It seems to be in very high demand. . . ." Verbena continued, adding a comment that Pam couldn't make out.

". . . PRISONER!" Pam heard a moment later.

At that, Pam leaned in closer to the door, determined to learn more. But then she STUMBLED on her bucket, and it fell over with a crash.

The squeaking stopped immediately, and the two rodents rushed to the door. Pam was AMAZED by how similar they looked. They had to be sisters! And there was something else. . . .

The mouse who had just arrived was the **mysterious** rodent she and her friends had been following!

"What are you doing here?" Verbena asked angrily. "Go clean somewhere else!"

Pam nodded and TOOK OFF in silence. As she rounded the corner, she heard the two rodents saying, "Let's go check." Pam turned around just in time to GLiMPSE Verbena and the other rodent heading into the laboratory, where her friends were hiding.

I hope they don't find Colette, Nicky, and Paulina. . . . Those two sisters make MY FUR STAND ON END*!* Pam thought.

Colette, Nicky, and Paulina **exchanged** a worried look when they heard the lab door open. But fortunately, the laboratory was full of tables, carts, and shelves, so it was easy to HIDE.

Nicky peeked out just in time to see Verbena coming into the lab, ACCOMPANIED by the rodent they'd followed on the boat.

"If he still refuses to help us, we must take MATTERS into our own paws!" Verbena announced, heading toward the back of the LAB.

The two rodents approached a painting of a BLACK TULIP hanging on the back wall. They pushed the painting to one side, and the wall opened. The lab led to a *SECRET PASSAGE*! Colette, Nicky, and Paulina gestured to one another frantically. Before the passage could close again, they *quickly* squeezed in behind the two rodents.

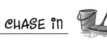
On the other side of the wall, there was a long, shadowy corridor. The mouselets shivered as the door closed behind them with a *HISS*.

 Why does the laboratory at the Black Tulip lead to a secret passageway? Are the two rodents with red fur hiding something?

THE SECRET HYBRID

The passageway led to a long staircase. At the bottom they spied a large metal door with a round **WINDOW** in the middle.

Colette, Nicky, and Paulina followed the rodents, trying not to attract **attention**.

As they drew closer to the door, Nicky spotted a scarf with black and green STRIPES lying on a chair. "That's **CASPER'S** scarf! He's wearing it in the PHOTO Jan showed us," she whispered.

The mouselets tried to go down the stairs slowly, staying close to the wall.

Verbena pulled a key out of her jacket

pocket. Just then, Nicky put her paw on a creaky step.

Verbena **spun around**, taking the mouselets by surprise. *"Who are you?!"*

"What are you doing here?!" the other rodent added.

"We're here to **UNCOVER** the truth," Nicky said boldly.

"We're looking for Casper van Garten,

Oops . . .

Tell us the truth!

who DISAPPEARED two days ago," Colette said. "It seems that this rodent here was the last to see him. When we went to the **flower market** to ask about him, she ran away."

"And we keep finding items that belong to Casper: his bookmark, his scarf . . ." Paulina continued. "We think that he might be here, and that you're keeping him **hidden** for some reason."

"How dare you trespass on our PRIVATE PROPERTY and make these crazy accusations!" the second rodent demanded. "You don't have a lick of **PROOF**! Now get out of here before we call the police. You have no right to stick your **SNOUTS** in our private business!"

"I don't think the police will see it that way, once we tell them everything we've discovered," Colette said.

"But . . . don't . . ." Verbena stammered.

The other rodent's expression changed at Colette's words. She put a **paw** on Verbena's shoulder.

It's time we confessed!

"It's okay, dear sister. We can't hide the truth any longer. There's too much evidence against us. It's time we confessed and took them to our PRISONER. I'll take the fall for both of us — this whole thing was my idea to begin with."

"Are you sure, Iris?" Verbena said, dumbfounded. "Well, if you say so . . ."

"Please, come with us. As you can see, Casper is down here!" Iris said, opening the door and gesturing for Colette, Nicky, and Paulina to come **inside**.

"Casper!" Paulina exclaimed. Without **hesitation**, the mouselets rushed into the cell to join Jan's dad.

By the time they realized their mistake, it was too late. The **heavy** iron door was closing behind them, IMPRISONING the mouselets along with Casper!

Paulina scurried back to the door. "OPEN UP!" she shouted.

Identical evil grins appeared on the two sisters' snouts. "You thought you were brainier than bookmice, didn't you? But you took the cheese and walked right into our trap!" Iris said triumphantly.

"You only pretended to be sorry!" Nicky shouted.

"Obviously!" Verbena sneered. "Do you honestly think we'd give up so easily on the BIGGEST DEAL of our lives?"

"What in the name of cheese are you squeaking about?" Nicky asked.

"The tulip bulb that this gentlemouse came up with. He won't share the **CREATION PROCESS**!

"My sister, Iris, and I deal in rare varieties of tulips, and for years we've been searching for a special bulb like the one Casper created. A specimen like his would make a fortune for any flower dealer!"

"But this stubborn rodent has refused all our offers. He won't sell it to us!" her sister hissed.

"So we had only one option left. . . ." Verbena continued.

"**STEALING IT!** But we weren't able to find the bulb. . . . Casper has hidden it well, and he won't tell us anything."

"I'll never tell you the secret of my

hybrid!" Jan's father cried. "You just want to get rich off my discovery. But I want to share my creation with the world! Everyone should be able to draw **inspiration** from my tulip."

Iris snorted. "You're nothing but a dim-witted **dreamer**, Casper!"

"At least I've held on to my dreams!" Casper retorted. "You, on the other paw, have turned into a money-grubbing pack rat! You've **traded** your hopes and dreams for a shot at riches and power!"

"Dreams? Those were just the **stupid illusions** of a young mouselet! Now I know what really counts." Iris sniffed.

"Are you sure about that?" Casper shot back.

Iris **stormed away** without replying. Her sister followed her.

A TALE
FROM THE PAST

The cell was silent for a moment, and then Casper sighed. "I'm sorry that you fell into this TRAP. How did you found me here?"

Paulina answered. "We're **friends** of Jan's. He's been looking everywhere for you."

I'm sorry!

CASPER covered his snout with his paws.

"I'm heartbroken that you and Jan got mixed up in all this. It's all my fault! I never suspected Iris and her sister would turn out to be so greedy. . . ."

"You've known them for a while?" Colette asked.

The botanist nodded. "Iris and I went to college together. In those days, she was different. We were CLOSE friends. Iris

Casper

Iris

was always very ambitious, but I never dreamed her aspirations would take such a dark turn!"

"Have you and Iris been in touch since then?" Nicky asked.

"No. We had a falling out. It happened after we were given a project in class to do in pairs: We had to grow **rare flowers** and study their development.

"I was intrigued by the project, but Iris was obsessed. She wanted us to get the highest grade in the class, and she was determined to get our work PUBLISHED. So she cheated and resorted to using a banned FERTILIZER.

When I discovered what she'd done, I withdrew our names from the competition. She's never forgiven me for that."

"And that was the end of your friendship?" Paulina asked.

"Yes, just like that, we stopped squeaking. We hadn't seen each other for almost twenty years. Then, a few months ago, she got in touch with me again. She told me that she had started a flower-selling business with her sister. . . ."

"THE BLACK TULIP!"

"Exactly. I was SURPRISED but pleased to hear from her. As soon as I told her about my tulip, Iris wanted to meet me in the fur. I thought that she was just interested in my work, but when we met at the flower market, she told me her plans. She was proud of what a good businessmouse she'd become, and she proposed that she acquire my creation.

"I refused right away, so she invited me out to her office to show me her business. Out of friendship, I agreed to come with her. But Iris just wanted to distract me while her sister searched my greenhouse for the **bulb**. . . ."

"She didn't find it, right?"

"No, she didn't find it, because —"

"**AAAAAAAAAAAAH!**"

A shout suddenly filled the air. Then there was a series of metallic clicks and thuds.

BANG! BAM! BONG!

Colette, Nicky, and Paulina leaped to their paws. But a fraction of a second later, they heard a familiar squeak. . . .

"Have no fear, mouselets! Your sister Pam is here!"

PAM THE HERO!

After she saw Iris and Verbena enter the laboratory, Pam had waited a few minutes so she wouldn't be spotted. Then she had slipped into the lab . . . and found it empty!

"What? Where did those two DISAPPEAR to?!" she mumbled, searching every corner of the large room. Her **friends** were gone, too. Luckily she noticed an object shining on the floor.

"Greasy cat guts! That's Paulina's MousePad!"

The MousePad was lying near a **WALL** with a painting of a tulip on it.

Pam thought it must have fallen out of her friend's backpack, maybe while she was hiding or *running* away. "Strange, though.

It's Paulina's MousePad!

What was she doing all the way over here? There's **NO** door in this wall," Pam whispered. She instinctively drew closer to the painting to straighten it when ... CLICK!

With a sudden lurch, the wall opened, revealing the SECRET PASSAGE.

Pam heard squeaks coming from down below. Quiet as a mouse, she scurried down the stairs.

When she reached the bottom, she spotted the two rodents with RED FUR standing in front of a large door. Through the door's window, she could see the shapes of her friends and an older rodent.

Pam ducked into the SHADOWS, her heart beating fast. Then the two sisters turned to go back up the stairs. Verbena had a large bunch of keys and a **sinister** smile on her snout.

Moldy mozzarella! I need to do something to free my friends, Pam thought. She sprang into action *faster* than a rat chased by a cat.

Pam **flattened** herself against the wall. Then she stuck out the mop she'd brought with her.

The TWO SISTERS were so busy discussing their predicament, they didn't notice. They

tripped on the mop and sprawled across the floor!

Pam took advantage of the element of surprise. Before the sisters could get up again, she tied their paws using a FIRE hose attached to the wall. Then she grabbed Verbena's key ring.

"What in the name of string cheese do you think you're doing?!" Verbena

shouted. She was madder than a cat with a bad case of fleas.

"I'm here to free my friends and **Casper** from your clutches!" cried Pam. She rushed to help her friends.

Hooray!

"Hooray, Pam!" Colette exclaimed, hugging her friend. "How did you do it?!"

"It was easy. I just had to straighten a painting," Pam replied, shrugging.

"Okay, this reunion has been nice, but now let's get out of here! This place makes my fur crawl," said Nicky. She hated tight spaces.

"Yes, but first let's make a plan," Colette said, pointing to the two sisters, who were still tied up with the hose and were fuming furiously.

"You're just meddling little mouselets! Free us immediately!" Verbena exclaimed.

"I have a better idea," Casper said. "Why don't we give you a little time to reflect on what you've done, down here where it's peaceful? The police will be here soon enough. What do you say, mouselets?"

"That sounds like a GREAT IDEA!" exclaimed Pam.

After shutting the two sisters up in the underground chamber, the Thea Sisters and Jan's father headed for the SECRET PASSAGE.

Once they were safely out of the LAB and the office building, the mouselets caught their breaths and explained everything they'd discovered to Pam.

"**Verbena** and Iris would do anything to get their paws on Casper's **creation**," Paulina began.

"That's *right*," Colette said. "They wanted to make the **BLACK TULIP** rich."

Casper shook his snout. "I worked for years on that **hybrid**. It's the fruit of all my research, and I couldn't let it end up in the paws of unscrupulous rodents. That's why I **HID** it. I was afraid that something like this would happen!"

"But where did you hide it?" Pam asked, scratching her snout.

Casper smiled. "In a very safe place. But I'm sure that my son has found it! And tonight, maybe he will present it to the committee for me. . . ."

"Squeaking of which — Jan and Violet!" Paulina exclaimed. "We **ABSOLUTELY** must let them know that we found Casper! By this time, they might have gone to the police. Now, where did I put . . ."

"Are you looking for **THIS**?" Pam said, pawing over the MousePad. "Luckily, I found it. And it helped me find you!"

Paulina took a **picture** of Casper smiling and sent it to Violet along with a message.

AN UNEXPECTED MESSAGE

MEANWHILE, Violet and Jan were deciding what to do next. The mouselet had tried to **call** her friends several times, but there was no response.

"**I don't understand**... maybe they're

We need to go!

in a place with no service," she said after her last try.

"It doesn't matter. My father has been **MISSING** for too long. It's time to report his disappearance to the police," said Jan seriously.

"At least we saved the **bulb**," Violet said, looking at the small box resting in front of her.

"Let's take it with us, along with the **file** of photos my father prepared. We'll go to the police station and then directly to the **DUTCH BOTANIC COMMITTEE**. They're expecting my father, but I'll go in his place. The **BULB** is so important to him — I can't let this **opportunity** go to waste."

Violet nodded. She pawed Jan the small box with the **bulb** and the materials. Just as they were on the doorstep, ready to leave, she felt her cell phone **vibrate** with an incoming message.

We'll see you at the committee in two hours!

"It's from Colette, Nicky, Pam, and Paulina! They did it!" Violet exclaimed. "They found your father!"

"Thank goodmouse! I — I can hardly believe it. . . ." Jan faltered. There were **tears** in his eyes. His father was safe with his new **friends**, and soon they would be reunited!

TOGETHER AGAIN

The DUTCH BOTANIC COMMITTEE was made up of nine of the most distinguished experts in their field. The group had gathered at the town hall. They were all enthusiastic about seeing the bulb Casper had created.

An older rodent approached one of his colleagues. "I can't wait to evaluate Van Garten's new creation. It's bound to be something very special."

It will be something special!

"I agree," she replied. "My CURIOSITY is killing me!"

"Well then," proposed

another colleague, "let's call in Casper van Garten."

When he opened the door to the waiting room, the botanist found himself snout-to-snout with a ratlet and a mouselet.

Jan and Violet had **arrived** promptly at the Dutch Botanic Committee meeting, with the **PRECIOUS BOX** held tightly in their paws. They were waiting anxiously for Jan's father and their friends, who were still nowhere to be **seen**.

"Where is Casper van Garten? And who are you?" the BOTANIST asked.

Jan stepped forward. "My name is Jan van Garten. I'm Casper's son. My father is . . . um, he's been **delayed**, but I'm sure he'll be here any moment. With your permission, I'd like to begin the presentation of my father's **hybrid**."

"Of course. It's a pleasure to meet Casper's son," the professor replied cordially. "Please, come in."

Jan and Violet entered the room and settled themselves **in front** of the committee.

"Go on, young Van Garten. Tell us about your father's work!" said the professor.

"Um, okay. Well you see, he's been working on a very special BULB that . . . um . . ."

The committee started to murmur.

Jan cleared his throat, but before he could continue, the door opened behind him.

Papa!

"I think I can take it from here," Casper declared.

"Papa!" Jan exclaimed, running to greet his father, who had entered the room with Colette, Nicky, Pam, and Paulina.

Jan hugged his father warmly, while Violet rushed over to see her friends.

"What happened? And where did you find Casper?" she asked.

"That story is longer than a cat's tail, Vi," Colette told her. "We'll tell you everything when we have a moment, but now we have something more important to do."

"Yes! I need to tell everyone about my **tulip**!" Casper said.

Casper's presentation of his **hybrid** left the committee squeakless. The botanists listened with admiration as he described how he'd managed to create **PINK** and **yellow** stripes and the perfect shape of the petals on his tulip.

When the committee retreated to judge the tulip properly, the mouselets took the opportunity to **share** everything that had happened at the Black Tulip offices.

"What a bunch of crooked cheddarheads!"

Jan exclaimed. "Why, those rodents are greedier than my great-great-aunt Miserly Moneymouse! I can't believe they kidnapped you."

"Actually, they didn't want me, only my bulb," Casper explained.

"That makes sense," said Violet. "It was a **BRILLIANT IDEA** to hide it in Vincent's room."

"Who's Vincent?" Pam asked.

Violet, Jan, and Casper exchanged a look and started to **laugh**.

"Pam, I'll fill you in later. Look, the committee is returning!"

All the **BOTANISTS** took their places around the conference table, while the committee **chairmouse** remained standing. "Professor Casper van Garten, this committee proclaims your **bulb** to be qualified, and we have unanimously decided to include it among the most **distinguished** varieties at our botanic center," he declared.

The news was greeted with **DEAFENING** applause, which let up only when the professor continued, "It's with great joy that we announce our decision to call this new tulip hybrid 'Casper van Garten' in honor of its **cReatoR**!"

The Thea Sisters put their paws around Jan's father, who was wiping away tears of joy.

Then Casper found his squeak. "Thank you all, from the bottom of my **heart**! It's a great honor for me to receive this recognition from the DUTCH BOTANIC COMMITTEE. I've **dedicated** my whole life to flowers. I've always believed that their precious beauty should be shared by all. But I didn't get here on my own.

"I must give special thanks to my son, Jan, and his friends. Without their COURAGE, I would never have received this honor."

Now it was the THEA SISTERS' turn to wipe tears of joy from their eyes!

THANK YOU ALL, FROM THE BOTTOM OF MY HEART!

A MARVEMOUSE SURPRISE

The adventure in Holland wasn't over yet. The next **MORNING**, a marvemouse surprise awaited the Thea Sisters.

When they left town hall the night before, Jan **announced** that he wanted to take the mouselets somewhere special, but he had been very mysterious about where.

As soon as she woke up in the morning, Colette **burst** into the kitchen of the youth hostel where the Thea Sisters were staying. She was still in her **PaJaMas**.

"Rotten rats' teeth, what am I going to do?!"

"What's wrong, Colette?" asked Paulina, who was eating **BREAKFAST** with Pam.

"How can I choose what to wear if I don't know where we're going?!"

"Oh, Colette, this is more serious than a seven-cheese pizza," said Pam, rolling her eyes. "What a terrible **problem**!"

"I'm glad you understand! I don't know if I should wear my **PINK** dress with high heels, or a more casual outfit with ballet flats."

Fancy or casual?

What a terrible problem!

Pam and Paulina exchanged a look and said TOGETHER, "We vote for the casual outfit!"

Colette scurried out of the room. "I'll be ready faster than you can squeak, 'fabumouse fashionista'!"

Fifteen minutes later, the Thea Sisters stepped outside the hostel and found Jan waiting for them in his **VAN**.

"Good morning, mouselets. Hop in!"

"Aren't you going to tell us where we're **going**?" Paulina asked, taking a seat in the back.

"No, it's a **SURPRISE**," he said. "And anyway, words couldn't do it justice. You have to see it with your own **EYES**."

Soon the group reached Noordwijk*.

Jan **PARKED** the van and announced, **"We're here!"**

A crowd of rodents streamed through the main street. The Thea Sisters joined the throng.

Suddenly, at the end of the street, the **enormouse shape** of a pink-and-white castle appeared. It was as if they had stepped into a **fairy tale**!

* Noordwijk is a town in southern Holland famous for its flower festival.

"How **beautiful**!" Colette exclaimed. "But . . . is it made of . . ."

"Flowers!" Jan said, nodding. "Today is the biggest flower parade in all of Holland.

"For the past few days, teams of rodents have been covering these floats with flowers for the parade."

"Look, there's Cinderella's coach!" Paulina exclaimed.

Jan nodded and smiled. "Every year there is a **special theme** for the decorations. The theme this year, as you can see, is FAIRY TALES!"

Pam was following a float that looked like the gingerbread house from *Hansel and Gretel*.

"**CHEESY CRUMB CAKES!**" the mouselet exclaimed. "It's so realistic I'm starting to drool! Too bad you can't eat it . . ."

"That's where you're wrong, Pam," Jan replied. "Tonight, we are going to feast on **Flowers**!"

The mouselets looked at him with surprise. **"What do you mean?"**

"My father is expecting you for dinner, and for this **special** occasion he's prepared a series of dishes that feature flowers and their petals. You'll see how **DELICIOUS** they can be," Jan promised.

The mouselets followed the parade all day long, enchanted by the fabumouse colors and the **FANTASTIC** shapes of the parade floats. They worked up quite an appetite for that evening's flower feast!

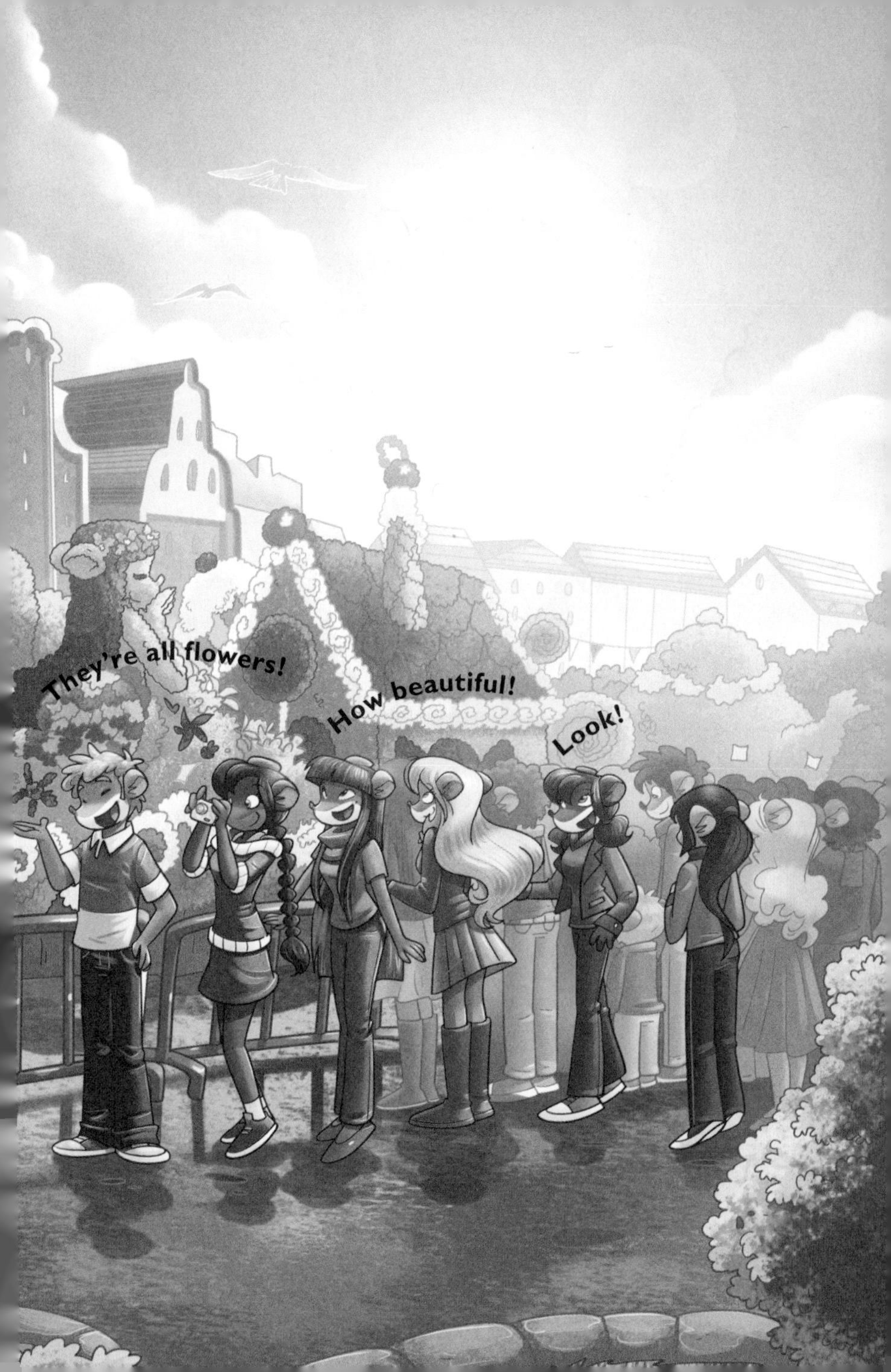
They're all flowers!
How beautiful!
Look!

PETALS ON THE PLATE

As soon as they arrived at Jan's house, the mouselets were overwhelmed by a delicious aroma. Casper had written out the menu he'd prepared for the evening. It listed all the FLORAL dishes the Thea Sisters would be tasting.

Acacia flower pasta

❀

Fried tulips

❀

Rose and magnolia frittata

Dinner was delectable! At the end of the meal, the mouselets were stuffed.

"Would you like to go for one last WALK?" Jan suggested, glancing at Violet.

"That sounds nice. I'd love to stretch my paws," said Violet.

"You go ahead," said Colette. "Paulina and I have a few questions we want to ask Casper."

"You'd have to roll me like a wheel of cheese after everything I ate!" groaned Pam. "I'm going to hang out here."

"And I want to stay here and play with Vincent," said Nicky. She loved animals.

Jan smiled. "Okay, we'll be back soon!" He and Violet headed outside.

"The weeks have FLOWN by," said Violet as they walked along. "I can hardly believe we're leaving for Whale Island tomorrow."

"I know," Jan agreed. "It seems like just yesterday you walked into the Studio for the first time. You were late and feeling GRUMPY, of course!"

"You know me, I'm just not a morning mouse!" said Violet, laughing. "I had to Recover from the flight here." Then she grew SERIOUS. "With everything that's happened in the last few days, I've almost forgotten it's time to GO."

"I didn't forget," Jan replied, stopping her. "I made SOMETHING for you." He pulled a sheet of drawing paper from his pocket and pawed it to Violet.

Violet was struck squeakless for a moment. "It — it's me," she stuttered at last. "Oh, Jan, how nice!"

Her friend SMiLeD. "I've gotten to KNOW you well over these last few weeks. I know that you're a bit of a perfectionist, that you can't survive without sleep, and that when you're angry, I'm in trouble! But I've also learned that you are the truest, most loyal friend a mouse could want. I tried to EXPRESS all this in your portrait."

Violet was moved. "Will you come see us at Mouseford?" she asked.

"Of course! And in the meantime, let's email each other and share our sketches. Okay?" Jan said.

"You bet," said Violet, SMILING. "After everything

we've been through, you're practically an **HONORARY** Thea Sister by now. Squeaking of the Thea Sisters, I'm so glad they were able to join me here. It's been a marvemouse adventure!"

THEY WERE MORE THAN FRIENDS. THEY WERE SISTERS!

Thea Sisters

Don't miss these exciting Thea Sisters adventures!

Thea Stilton and the Dragon's Code

Thea Stilton and the Mountain of Fire

Thea Stilton and the Ghost of the Shipwreck

Thea Stilton and the Secret City

Thea Stilton and the Mystery in Paris

Thea Stilton and the Cherry Blossom Adventure

Thea Stilton and the Star Castaways

Thea Stilton: Big Trouble in the Big Apple

Thea Stilton and the Ice Treasure

Thea Stilton and the Secret of the Old Castle

Thea Stilton and the Blue Scarab Hunt

Thea Stilton and the Prince's Emerald

Thea Stilton and the Mystery on the Orient Express

Thea Stilton and the Dancing Shadows

Thea Stilton and the Legend of the Fire Flowers

Thea Stilton and the Spanish Dance Mission

Thea Stilton and the Journey to the Lion's Den

Thea Stilton and the Great Tulip Heist

Up Next!

Thea Stilton and the Chocolate Sabotage

Check out these very special editions featuring me and the Thea Sisters!

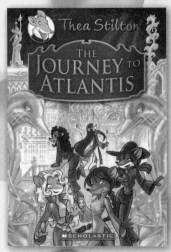

THE JOURNEY
TO ATLANTIS

THE SECRET OF
THE FAIRIES

MEET
GERONIMO STILTONIX

He is a spacemouse — the Geronimo Stilton of a parallel universe! He is captain of the spaceship *MouseStar 1*. While flying through the cosmos, he visits distant planets and meets crazy aliens. His adventures are out of this world!

#1 Alien Escape

#2 You're Mine, Captain!

Be sure to read all my fabumouse adventures!

#1 Lost Treasure of the Emerald Eye

#2 The Curse of the Cheese Pyramid

#3 Cat and Mouse in a Haunted House

#4 I'm Too Fond of My Fur!

#5 Four Mice Deep in the Jungle

#6 Paws Off, Cheddarface!

#7 Red Pizzas for a Blue Count

#8 Attack of the Bandit Cats

#9 A Fabumouse Vacation for Geronimo

#10 All Because of a Cup of Coffee

#11 It's Halloween, You 'Fraidy Mouse!

#12 Merry Christmas, Geronimo!

#13 The Phantom of the Subway

#14 The Temple of the Ruby of Fire

#15 The Mona Mousa Code

#16 A Cheese-Colored Camper

#17 Watch Your Whiskers, Stilton!

#18 Shipwreck on the Pirate Islands

#19 My Name Is Stilton, Geronimo Stilton

#20 Surf's Up, Geronimo!

#21 The Wild, Wild West

#22 The Secret of Cacklefur Castle

A Christmas Tale

#23 Valentine's Day Disaster

#24 Field Trip to Niagara Falls

#25 The Search for Sunken Treasure

#26 The Mummy with No Name

#27 The Christmas Toy Factory

#28 Wedding Crasher

#29 Down and Out Down Under

#30 The Mouse Island Marathon

#31 The Mysterious Cheese Thief

Christmas Catastrophe

#32 Valley of the Giant Skeletons

#33 Geronimo and the Gold Medal Mystery

#34 Geronimo Stilton, Secret Agent

#35 A Very Merry Christmas

#36 Geronimo's Valentine

#37 The Race Across America

#38 A Fabumouse School Adventure

#39 Singing Sensation

#40 The Karate Mouse

#41 Mighty Mount Kilimanjaro

#42 The Peculiar Pumpkin Thief

#43 I'm Not a Supermouse!

#44 The Giant
Diamond Robbery

#45 Save the White
Whale!

#46 The Haunted
Castle

#47 Run for the Hills,
Geronimo!

#48 The Mystery in
Venice

#49 The Way of
the Samurai

#50 This Hotel Is
Haunted

#51 The Enormouse
Pearl Heist

#52 Mouse in Space!

#53 Rumble in
the Jungle

#54 Get into Gear,
Stilton!

#55 The Golden
Statue Plot

#56 Flight of the
Red Bandit

The Hunt for the
Golden Book

#57 The Stinky
Cheese Vacation

Don't miss my journey through time!

Be sure to read all my adventures in the Kingdom of Fantasy!

THE KINGDOM OF FANTASY

THE QUEST FOR PARADISE:
THE RETURN TO THE KINGDOM OF FANTASY

THE AMAZING VOYAGE:
THE THIRD ADVENTURE IN THE KINGDOM OF FANTASY

THE DRAGON PROPHECY:
THE FOURTH ADVENTURE IN THE KINGDOM OF FANTASY

THE VOLCANO OF FIRE:
THE FIFTH ADVENTURE IN THE KINGDOM OF FANTASY

Meet
GERONIMO STILTONOOT

He is a cavemouse—Geronimo Stilton's
ancient ancestor! He runs the stone
newspaper in the prehistoric village
of Old Mouse City. From dealing with
dinosaurs to dodging meteorites,
his life in the Stone Age is full
of adventure!

#1 The Stone of Fire

#2 Watch Your Tail!

#3 Help, I'm in Hot Lava!

#4 The Fast and
the Frozen

#5 The Great
Mouse Race

Meet
CREEPELLA VON CACKLEFUR

I, *Geronimo Stilton*, have a lot of mouse friends, but none as **spooky** as my friend CREEPELLA VON CACKLEFUR! She is an enchanting and MYSTERIOUS mouse with a pet bat named **Bitewing**. YIKES! I'm a real 'fraidy mouse, but even I think CREEPELLA and her family are AWFULLY fascinating. I can't wait for you to read all about CREEPELLA in these a-mouse-ly funny and **spectacularly spooky** tales!

#1 The Thirteen Ghosts

#2 Meet Me in Horrorwood

#3 Ghost Pirate Treasure

#4 Return of the Vampire

#5 Fright Night

#6 Ride for Your Life

THANKS FOR READING,
AND GOOD-BYE UNTIL OUR
NEXT ADVENTURE!

Thea Sisters